Ethan's 1st
Christmas
from Great-
Grandma
Marian
2008

Little Bunny's Sleepless Night
Story Carol Roth
Illustrations Valeri Gorbachev

Nicky and the Big, Bad Wolves
Story and Illustrations Valeri Gorbachev

Who Will Tuck Me in Tonight?
Story Carol Roth
Illustrations Valeri Gorbachev

ISBN-13: 978-1-4351-0465-5
ISBN-10: 1-4351-0465-X

Printed and bound in China
1 3 5 7 9 10 8 6 4 2

Bedtime Stories

NORTHSOUTH
BOOKS

TABLE OF CONTENTS

Little Bunny's Sleepless Night

Little Bunny had no brothers or sisters.
He had his very own room with his very own bed.
   But sometimes he got lonely—so lonely that he
couldn't fall asleep.
   One night he thought: What I need is the company
of a good friend.

So he hopped next door to his good friend Squirrel.
"May I sleep here tonight?"

"Of course," said Squirrel as he welcomed him in.
Tucked all snug in bed next to squirrel, Little Bunny
thought how lucky he was not to be alone.
"Good night, Squirrel," said Little Bunny.
"Good night, Little Bunny," answered his friend.

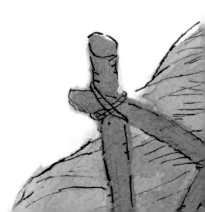

Falling asleep was easy, but staying asleep was not. Little Bunny was soon awakened by C-R-U-N-C-H, C-R-U-N-C-H, C-R-U-N-C-H!

"What's that noise?" he asked as he sat up in bed.

"It's just me cracking acorns," said Squirrel. "I always have a little snack in the middle of the night."

"Well, thanks for having me, but I can't sleep with all that noise!"

So Little Bunny left and hopped some more until he reached his good friend Skunk's house.

"May I sleep here tonight?"

"YES! YES! A HUNDRED TIMES YES!" shouted Skunk. "No one has ever asked to sleep over before!"

Afraid Little Bunny might change his mind, Skunk quickly pulled him inside.

"This is fun," Skunk said as they got into their beds.

Shortly after, they fell asleep . . . but not for long.

Little Bunny was soon awakened by a terrible smell.
"What smells?" he asked as he jumped up.
"I'm afraid I do," said Skunk. "I forgot someone else
was in my room. I got scared and sprayed."
"Well, thanks for having me, but I can't sleep with
that smell!"

So Little Bunny left and hopped some more until
he reached his good friend Porcupine.

"May I sleep here tonight?"

"Certainly," said Porcupine. "You take my bed and
I'll sleep on the floor."

"Yippee!" shouted Little Bunny as he climbed
into Porcupine's bed and bounced around with excitement.

"OUCH!" he screamed. "What do you
have in here?"

"It's just my quills," said Porcupine. "I lose
some every now and then."

"Well, thanks for having me, but I can't
sleep with those prickles!"

So Little Bunny left and hopped some more until
he reached his good friend Bear's place.

"May I sleep here tonight?"

"Why sure, make yourself at home," said Bear.

By now Little Bunny was so tired he just curled up
on the floor and went right to sleep.

But very soon after, Little Bunny was
Wakened by a loud rumbling noise.
Oh, no, it's thundering! he thought.
But it wasn't thundering at all. His friend
Bear was snoring!
"Well, I can't sleep with that snoring!"
said Little Bunny.

So he left and hopped some more until he reached
his good friend Owl's home.

"May I sleep here tonight?"

"Why yes, if you want to," said Owl. "Just follow me."

An exhausted Little Bunny went right to sleep,
But soon he was wakened by a bright light shining
in his eyes.

"PUT THE LIGHT OUT!" he shouted

"I can't," said Owl. "I stay up reading every night.
That's how I got to be so wise."

"Well, since you're so wise, could you please tell
me how I'm ever going to get some sleep?"

"That's easy," said Owl. Just go back home where
you belong."

Little Bunny took his wise friend's advice.
Too tired to hop, he dragged himself home.
His bed had never looked so good to him before.

He jumped right in.

"How wonderful!" he said to himself as he snuggled down. No crunching noise, no terrible smell, no prickly quills, no snoring, and no bright lights. Just me, by myself, and peace and quiet. Now I can fall asleep!"

And that's just what Little Bunny did!

Nicky
and the
Big, Bad Wolves

One windy night, Nicky woke up . . .

H-E-E-L-L-L-P!

Mother rushed right in
   "What on earth is the matter?" she asked.

"Wolves!" said Nicky. "A hundred wolves were chasing me!"

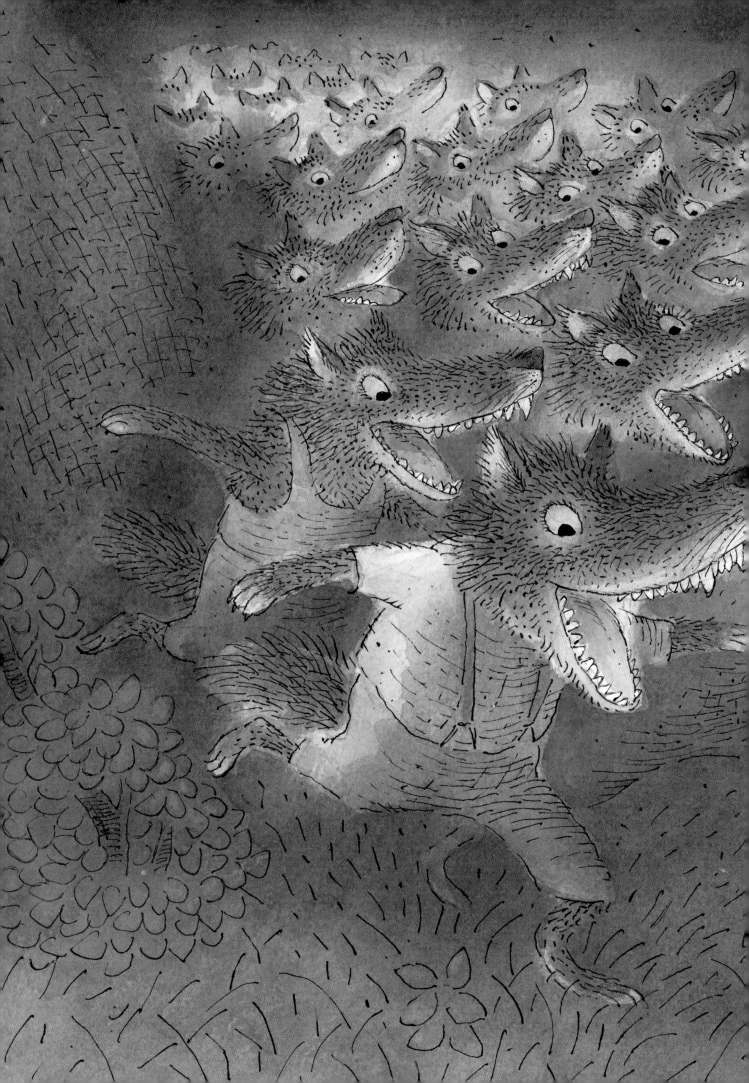

"A *hundred* wolves!" said Mother.
"Are you sure?"

44

"Well," said Nicky. "Maybe it was *fifty* wolves, but they were racing after me and I couldn't run away fast enough!"

"Fifty wolves!" said Mother. "Are you sure?"

"Well," said Nicky. "Maybe it was only *fifteen* wolves, but they were a bloodthirsty bunch."

49

"Fifteen wolves seems like a lot,"
said Mother. "Are you sure?"

"Well, maybe there were only *five*, actually," admitted Nicky. "But they were right on top of me!"

53

"It was just a bad dream, Nicky." said Mother. "And now it's time for you all to go back to sleep."

Mother tucked everyone in, turned out the light, and closed the door.

"Did you hear that?" said Nathan.
"It sounded like wolves!" said Nora.
"Hungry wolves!" said Ned.
"With huge fangs," said Nelly.

"And they're right outside!" said Nicky.

"*Now* what's the matter?" said Mother.

"A hundred wolves! Right outside our window! They're going to get us!"

"All of you, stay here," said Mother. "I'll settle this wolf business once and for all!"

"There now, said Mother. "Don't worry about those wolves. I chased them all away."

"Are you sure?" said Nicky.

"I'm sure!" said Mother. "But if they come back. I've got my broom right here to chase them away again."

So Nicky and his brothers and sisters all sniggled down and finally went to sleep—with Mother right in the middle!

Who Will Tuck Me in Tonight?

THE SUN WAS SETTING on the farm,
And Woolly, the little lamb, was sleepy.
But Woolly couldn't find his mother.
"Oh, who will tuck me in tonight?" he
asked sadly.

"I will, I will," said Mrs. Cow. "Don't you worry, I know how. Everything will be all right. I'll tuck you in real snug and tight."

Then Mrs. Cow spread out the blanket and
tucked Woolly in so tight that he couldn't move.

"*Stop!*" cried Woolly. "That's not right!
Oh, who will tuck me in tonight?"

"Fancy that," said Mrs. Cat,
"I can do it, just like that! I think
I know just what you're missing.
You need lots of bedtime kissing."

Then Mrs. Cat began to lick Woolly all over his face with her little tongue.

"*Yuck!*" cried Woolly. "That's not right!
Oh, who will tuck me in tonight?"

"Here I come," said Mrs. Horse. "I can do the job, of course. When you're in bed all nice and snug, I'll give you a great big hug."

Then Mrs. Horse sat down on Woolly's bed, wrapped herself around him, and squeezed with all her might.

"*Help!*" cried Woolly. "That's not right! Oh, who will tuck me in tonight?"

"No job's too small. No job's too big!
I can do it," said Mrs. Pig.
"Don't you move. I'll be right back.
I think you need a bedtime snack."

Then Mrs. Pig brought Woolly a pail
full of messy, stinky piggy snacks.

"*No, no!*" cried Woolly. "That's not right.
Oh, who will tuck me in tonight?"

"Don't you worry. You're in luck.
I can help," said Mrs. Duck.
"Don't you fret and don't you cry.
I'll sing a lovely lullaby."

Then Mrs. Duck sang, "*Quack, quack, quack . . .*
quack, quack, quack," but it didn't sound very
much like a lullaby to Woolly.

"*Enough!*" said Woolly. "That's not right.
Can't *anyone* tuck me in tonight!"

"I can!" said Mother Sheep.
"You're back!" cried Woolly.
"Yes, my little lamb. I'm so sorry I'm late."

She tucked his blanket in just right.
Not too loose and not too tight.

She gave him hugs and kisses, soft and sweet,
and something sensible to eat.

She sang some lovely lullabies, and
then little Woolly closed his eyes.